P9-DBY-261

1

Jumping Bean

Story and Pictures
by Edna Miller

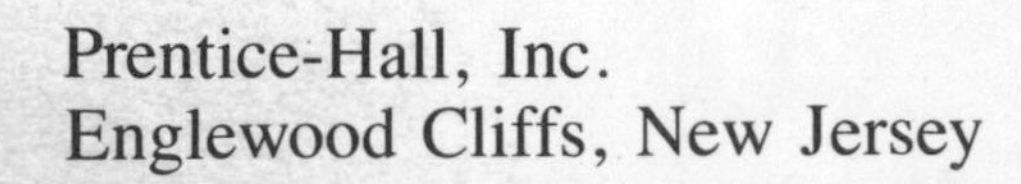

Prentice-Hall, Inc.
Englewood Cliffs, New Jersey

MEXICO

To Toni and Dan

Printed in the United States of America J
Prentice-Hall International, Inc., London
Prentice-Hall of Australia, Pty. Ltd., North Sydney
Prentice-Hall of Canada, Ltd., Toronto
Prentice-Hall of India Private Ltd., New Delhi
Prentice-Hall of Japan, Inc., Tokyo
Prentice-Hall of Southeast Asia Pte. Ltd., Singapore
Whitehall Books Limited, Wellington, New Zealand
1 2 3 4 5 6 7 8 9 10
Library of Congress Cataloging in Publication Data
Miller, Edna.
The jumping bean book.
SUMMARY: Many animals wonder at the bean that jumps.
In time its secret is revealed.
[1. Jumping bean–Fiction. 2. Animals–Fiction]
I. Title.
PZ7.M6128Ju [E] 79-15434
ISBN 0-13-512384-4

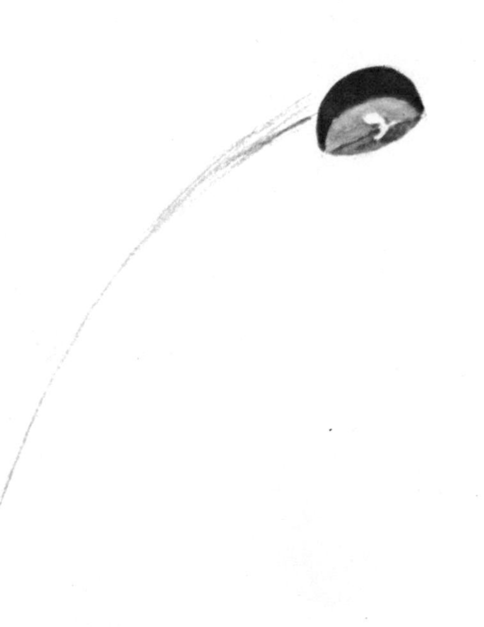

The ripe seed pods of the arrow plant popped
shooting round black seeds through the air.

One pod fell gently to the ground.
It rolled and hopped.
It tumbled sideways and backways
and around in circles.
The other seeds sprouted roots
to grow a new plant.

Not Jumping Bean!
There was something *else* alive inside.
Something that would make the little bean jump
for months in the hot desert sun.

When Jumping Bean found a shady spot
it would lie very still.

When the sun was high in the sky
Jumping Bean would leap . . .
though not as high as some other creatures
who lived at the desert's edge.

A grasshopper heard a clicking sound
as Jumping Bean hopped on loose stones.
"Are you a bug?" the grasshopper asked.
"What makes you jump?"

"You haven't legs like mine for leaping!"

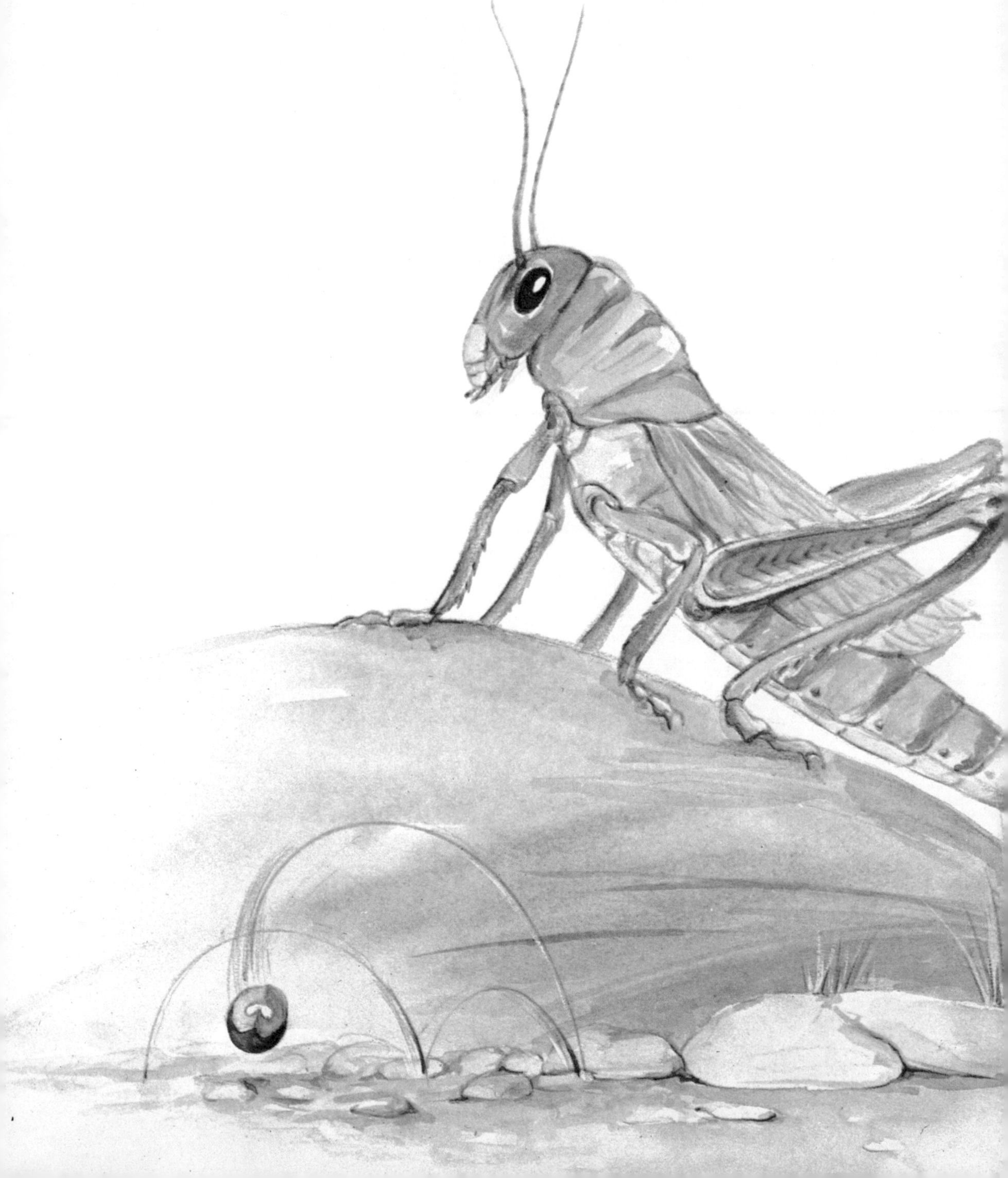

Jumping Bean didn't answer.
With a clickity-click and tap tap tap
it jumped to where the grasshopper sat.
It jumped to find a shady spot.

The grasshopper leaped away.

A toad heard the pattering sound
of rain on dry leaves.
When it leaped to find water
it found Jumping Bean instead.

The toad watched the bean for a while then asked.
"What is there inside you
that makes you jump that way?"

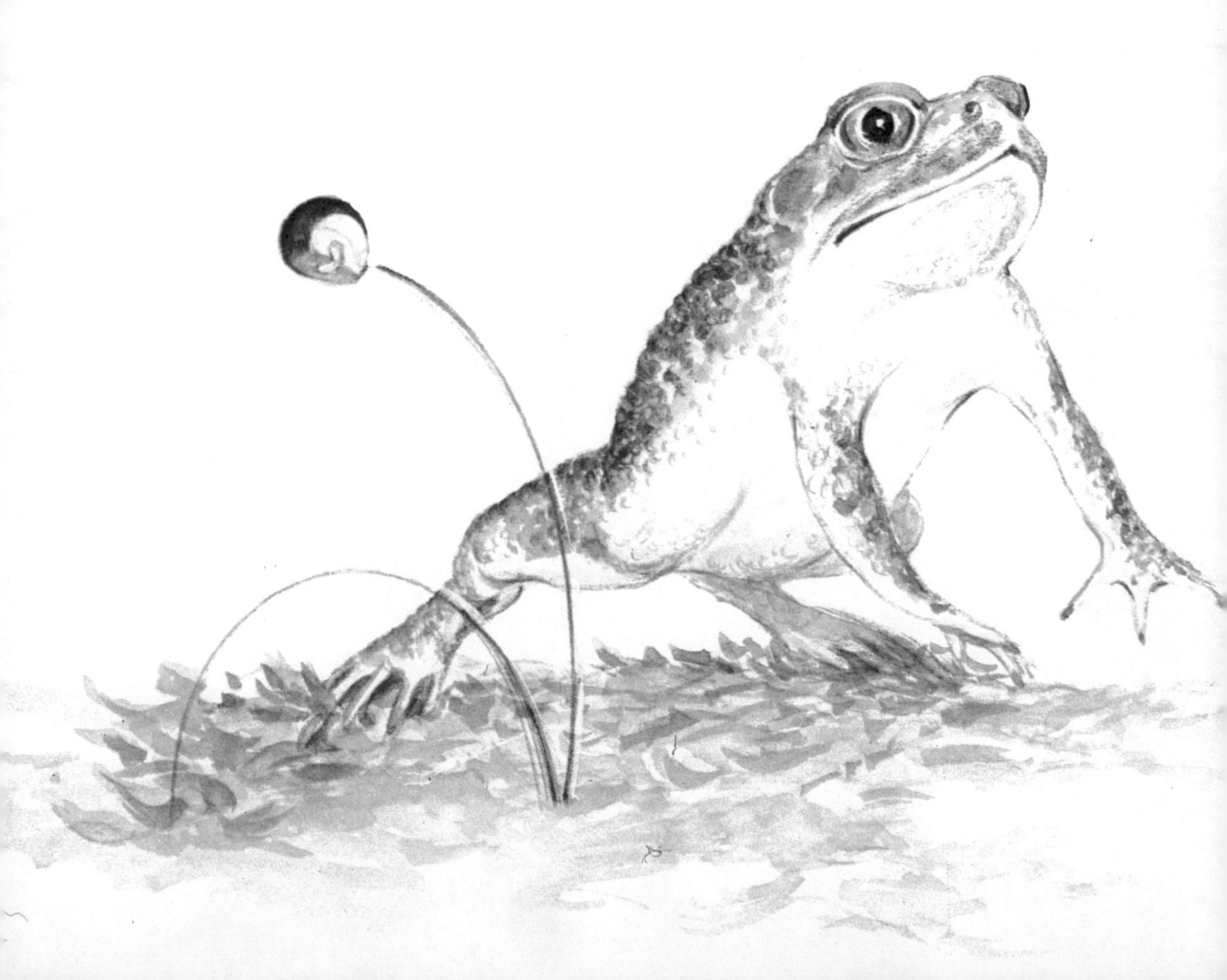

Jumping Bean didn't answer.
With a pit-pit pitter-pat
it hopped through the leaves toward the toad.
An insect would never do *that*!

The frightened toad leaped away.

A jumping mouse hunted seeds
to store beneath the ground.
With his cheeks full of seeds
and only room for one more
he reached for Jumping Bean.
When the mouse felt Jumping Bean
twitch in his paws
he dropped it to the ground.

Jumping Bean hopped on the hard desert floor.
Tic-tic-clickity-click.

The terrified mouse didn't wait to ask questions!

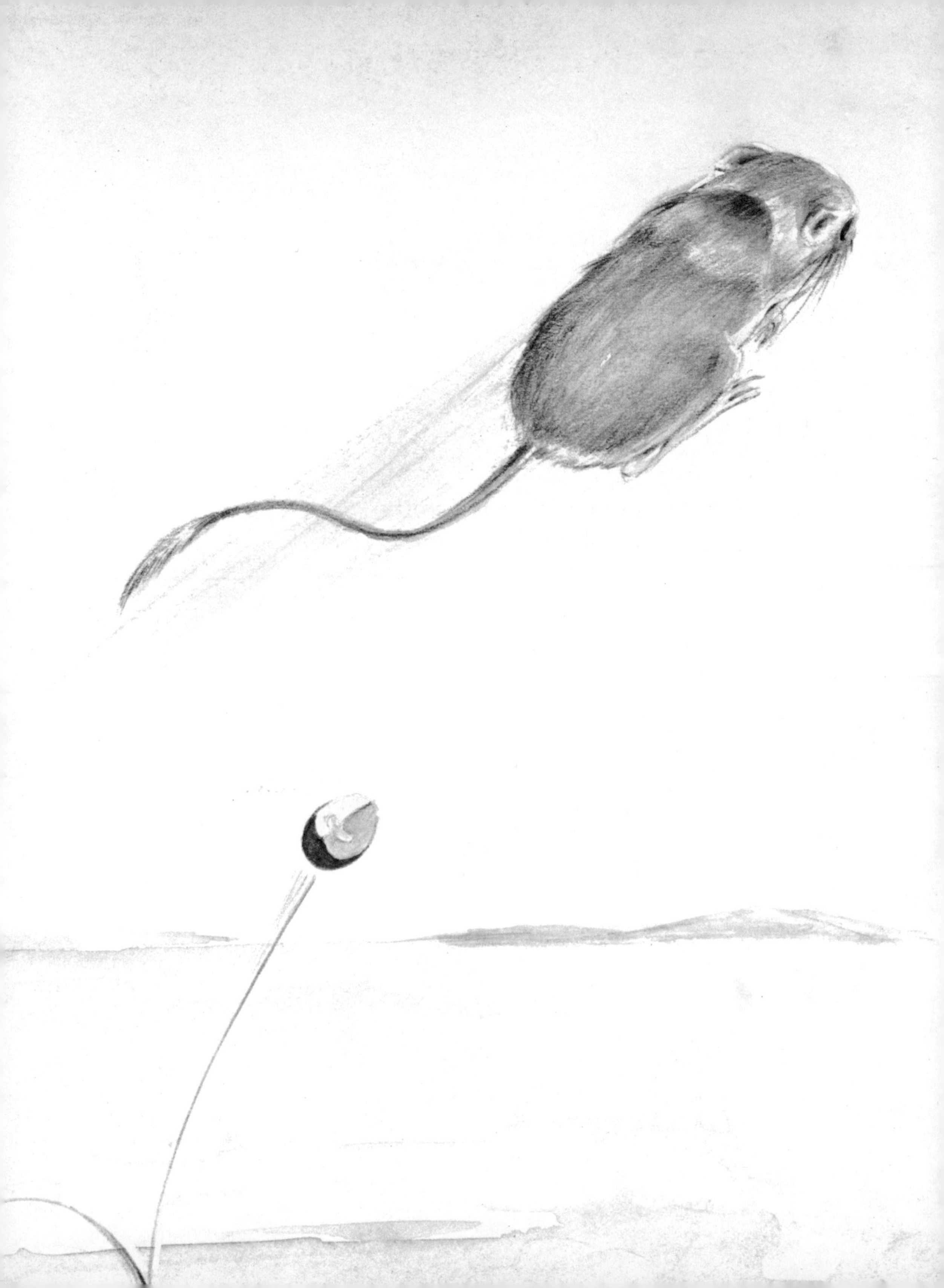

While a jackrabbit rested in the shade of a tree
he felt something jiggle beneath him.

The rabbit sprang to his feet in surprise.
Jumping Bean hopped from beneath him.
"Are you alive?" the rabbit asked.
"You have no eyes, ears, nose or mouth
and no long legs like mine for jumping."

Jumping Bean didn't answer.
It rolled over and over
then flipped in the air.

The jackrabbit bounded away.

One animal watched Jumping Bean
and did not jump away.
She knew what made the bean pod hop.
She knew a caterpillar lived in the bean
. . . a treat for a hungry wren.

The caterpillar sensed danger.
Hooking its feet to the bean's silken wall
the creature coiled like a spring.
Thrusting its body up and then down
it made its whole house jump away.

Wedged between stones
and safe from the wren
the caterpillar spun a cocoon around itself
and slept.
Its jumping days were over.

It was not until after
a heavy spring rain
that something stirred in Jumping Bean.
A small round door at the top of the bean
pushed slowly upward
and a pale gray form appeared.

On new born wings a tiny moth
flew past the sleeping wren
to lay its eggs on the blossoms
of the flowering arrow plant.